HOW THINGS ARE BUILT

Helen Edom

Edited by Janet Cook

Designed by Robert Walster and Chris Scollen

Illustrated by Guy Smith, Teri Gower and Chris Lyon

Consultant: Peter Wright BSc (Eng) Hons. C Eng M.I.C.E.

Contents

About building

This book shows you how buildings such as houses, roads and bridges are built.

On the right are some of the different sorts of builders you will meet in this book.

The person who makes walls out of bricks is called a bricklayer.

The person who makes things with wood is called a carpenter.

What are buildings made of?

Buildings are made out of strong things such as concrete, steel and wood. You can find out more about these on pages 22-23.

This diver dives into the sea to work on the underneath of an oil rig.

This person is called a welder. He uses a very hot tool to join metal pieces.

The story of building

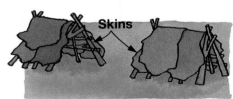

A million years ago, people built huts from branches. They hung animal skins over them to keep out rain.

Later, they moved blocks of stone by dragging them over tree trunks. They kept moving the trunks to the front of the stone.

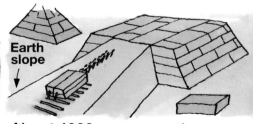

About 4000 years ago, the Egyptians built stone pyramids. They made earth slopes so they could drag stone blocks up to the top.

How buildings begin

Plan

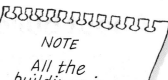

NOTE
All the buildings in this book can be built in many different ways. Usually only one way of building is shown.

Once somebody has had an idea for a building, a plan is drawn to show how it is to be built.

Engineers draw plans for buildings like bridges. They make sure these buildings don't fall down.

Architects draw plans for houses and offices. They work with engineers if the building is big.

Architects like to think of ways to make buildings attractive and pleasant to work in or live in.

When the plans are finished, a copy is given to the builders. The builders can then start.

Column

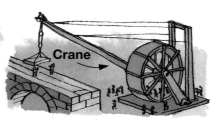

Crane

Over 2000 years ago, Greeks and Romans used stone columns to hold up buildings. The Romans are also famous for roads.

600 years ago, builders used cranes to lift loads. This helped them to build tall buildings like bridges and churches.

Now we have modern machines, twenty skyscrapers can be built in the same time that it took to build one pyramid.

3

Brick houses

Houses are built in many different ways. The builders you can see at work here and on the next two pages are building with bricks, concrete and wood. See if you can find out what your house is made from.

Preparing to build

The plan on the right shows what the house will look like and how big it is going to be.

Plan of house drawn by an architect.

1. The builders ▶ work out how many bricks and other things they need.

▲ 2. Lorries take everything to the site.

▲ 3. The builders measure out the site from the plans. They use string to mark the edges of the house.

The string is fixed to pieces of wood.

Trench filled with concrete.

Drain pipe

4. A concrete mixer mixes sand, cement, gravel and water to make concrete. ▼

Cement

Sand

▲ 5. A digger digs trenches between the string lines. These are filled with concrete to make a hard base (foundation). It also digs trenches for pipes.*

*Find out more about pipes on page 7.

4

Building the walls

Bricklayers build walls on the foundation. First they make the corners and put string between them. This helps them build straight.

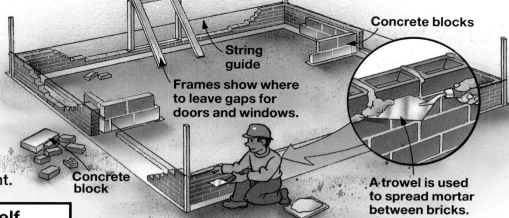

Concrete blocks

String guide

Frames show where to leave gaps for doors and windows.

Concrete block

A trowel is used to spread mortar between bricks.

The bricks are stuck together with mortar (see page 23).

The walls inside the house are made from big concrete blocks.

See for yourself

Try this experiment to see how important the damp-proof course is.

1. Dip some kitchen paper in water. The water goes up it.

Wet   Dry

2. Cut another piece in half. Tape the halves together with a small gap between them.

Tape

Gap

3. Dip it in water. The water cannot go above the waterproof tape.

Wet   Dry

Water goes up through floors and walls in this way, unless stopped by a waterproof layer.

Keeping water out of the house

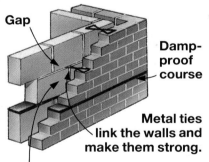

Gap

Damp-proof course

Metal ties link the walls and make them strong.

The air between the walls helps keep the house warm and dry.

◀ Another wall is built about 6cm inside the outer wall.

The bricklayer puts waterproof bitumenised felt (see page 22) in both walls, just above the ground. This stops water soaking up. It is called a damp-proof course.

Building the floor

The ground inside the ▶ walls is dug out. Concrete is poured over layers of stones, sand and plastic. The plastic stops water rising into the floor.

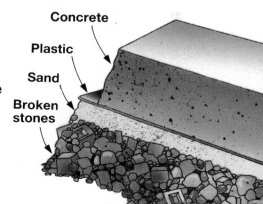

Concrete

Plastic

Sand

Broken stones

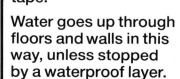

Building the upstairs

1. Builders lay pieces of wood (joists) from one wall to the other.

2. They nail wooden floorboards on top of the joists to make the floor.

Joists

Ceiling

Floorboards

Scaffolding

3. They nail plasterboards (see page 23) underneath the joists. This makes a ceiling for the downstairs rooms.

Scaffolding

Scaffolding is like a huge climbing frame made from steel tubes. Builders stand on planks laid across it to reach the top of the house.

Clamps are tightened around the tubes to fix them together.

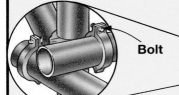

Bolt

Plasterboard

Houses with frames

The brick house on this page is held up by its walls. Other houses are held up by wooden, concrete or metal frames.

This often happens in the USA.

A wooden house which is held up by its frame can be moved on a lorry.

Wall

Frame

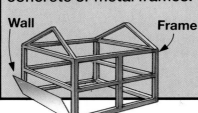

Upstairs rooms ▲

Plasterboards are used to divide the upstairs area into rooms.

Making the stairs ▶

The carpenter builds the staircase. The top of each step is called a tread. The upright pieces are called risers.

Putting the roof on

1. The frame for the roof is made from wooden triangular shapes. They rest on the walls.

2. Roofing felt is spread over the frame. Strips of wood are nailed on top.

3. Overlapping tiles are nailed to the strips. Rain runs off them and into the guttering.

Building the chimney

The chimney is built up through the roof. A metal strip (flashing) is bent round it. This stops rain leaking between the chimney and tiles.

The tiles used along the top are called ridge tiles.

Battens

Roofing felt

Guttering

Flashing

Floorboards

Riser

Tread

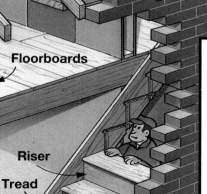

Finishing off

★ A glazier puts glass in the windows.
★ An electrician lays wiring.
★ A plasterer covers the walls with plaster.
★ A decorator paints the house.

Laying the water pipes

A plumber joins pipes together to carry water around the house.

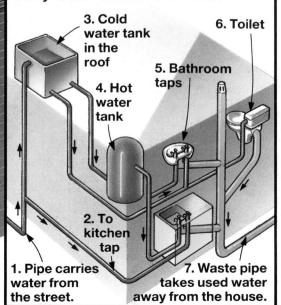

3. Cold water tank in the roof

6. Toilet

5. Bathroom taps

4. Hot water tank

2. To kitchen tap

1. Pipe carries water from the street.

7. Waste pipe takes used water away from the house.

Skyscrapers

A skyscraper is built on a huge frame. This is fixed to a strong base (foundation).

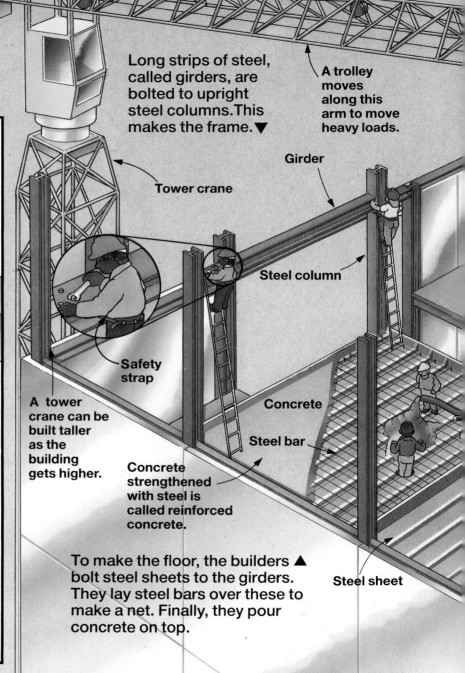

Skyscraper foundations

A skyscraper is very heavy, so it needs a strong foundation. It has legs, called piles, which go deep into the earth.

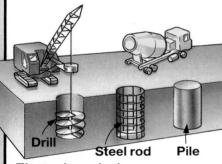

Drill **Steel rod** **Pile**

First, deep holes are ▲ drilled in the ground. Steel rods are put inside them. The holes are then filled with concrete.

Concrete bar

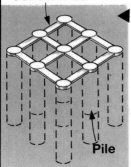

◄ The tops of the piles are joined with concrete bars. This is called a pile foundation.

Pile

Long strips of steel, called girders, are bolted to upright steel columns. This makes the frame. ▼

A trolley moves along this arm to move heavy loads.

Girder

Tower crane

Steel column

Safety strap

A tower crane can be built taller as the building gets higher.

Concrete

Steel bar

Concrete strengthened with steel is called reinforced concrete.

Steel sheet

To make the floor, the builders ▲ bolt steel sheets to the girders. They lay steel bars over these to make a net. Finally, they pour concrete on top.

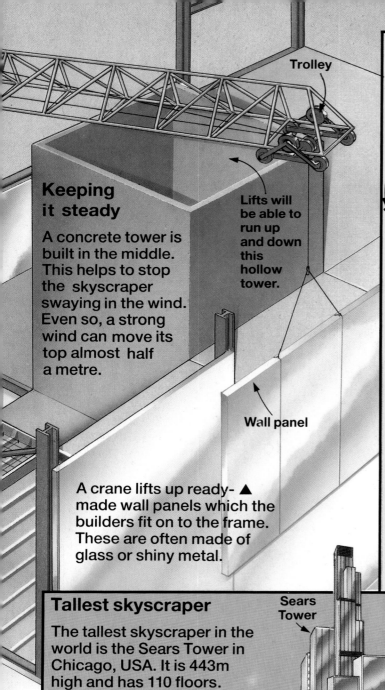

Trolley

Keeping it steady

A concrete tower is built in the middle. This helps to stop the skyscraper swaying in the wind. Even so, a strong wind can move its top almost half a metre.

Lifts will be able to run up and down this hollow tower.

Wall panel

A crane lifts up ready-△ made wall panels which the builders fit on to the frame. These are often made of glass or shiny metal.

Tallest skyscraper

The tallest skyscraper in the world is the Sears Tower in Chicago, USA. It is 443m high and has 110 floors.

Sears Tower

Build your own tower crane

1. Tie a short pencil ▶ on to a cotton reel (reel 1) with a rubber band.

Reel 1

Match

◀ 2. Slot reel 2 on the pencil. Fix a match* on this reel with plasticine.

Reel 2

3. Tie the end of a ▶ thread round reel 2. Tie the other end to a paper clip hook.

Thread

Hook

Tape

◀ 4. Tape a ruler on top of reel 1. Don't put any tape on the bottom of the reel.

5. Bend another ▶ clip around the ruler. Thread the hook through this clip.

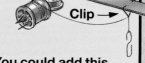

Clip →

Balance ruler with plasticine.

You could add this clip to help the thread wind easily.

Stick on matches* to make rests for the paper clip trolley.

Clean margarine tub

◀ 6. Slot reel 1 on a long pencil. Stand the pencil in reel 3. Wedge it inside a tub of stones and cover the tub with tape.

*Only use used matches.

9

Roads

Roads are made up of several layers. They need to be strong, because of all the cars and lorries which go over them every day.

Clearing the ground

1. First, the builders clear the ground. They cut down trees and use bulldozers to clear the bushes and stumps. ▶

Bulldozer

These are called caterpillar treads. They grip bumpy ground.

These little metal feet stamp on the ground to make it firm.

◀ 2. Machines called scrapers and excavators dig out the bumps and fill in the hollows.

Compactor

3. A large roller called a compactor is rolled over the ground to make it hard.

This scoop can swing round to dump the earth.

Scraper

Excavator

Blades scrape up the earth into this box.

Starting to build

Crushed rock is spread over the soil. A machine called a grader levels this stony layer.

Grader

Flattening hills

Steep roads are difficult to drive on. Builders make a hill less steep by cutting out earth at the top and piling it up at the bottom.

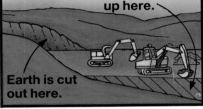

Earth is piled up here.

Earth is cut out here.

Finishing it off

1. Hot asphalt (see page 22) is poured into the front of a machine called a paver. The paver spreads it evenly over the road.

Paver

Asphalt comes out here.

Asphalt is used because it is soft when hot and gets hard as it goes cold.

Road roller

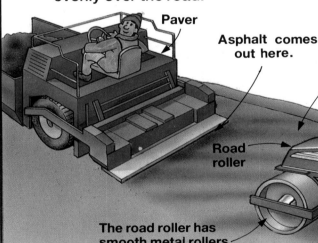

Record roads

The USA has the most roads (over six million kilometres). This length would go round the world 162 times.

The road roller has smooth metal rollers instead of wheels.

2. A heavy roller follows the paver. It presses the asphalt down, helping it to set hard.

3. Several layers of asphalt are put down. Stone chips are scattered on the top layer. These make the surface rough so car tyres will grip it safely.

Bridges

Bridges have to be very strong so that heavy lorries and trains can go across them.

On this page you can see how a bridge is built over a road.

1. First, concrete ledges (abutments) are built up on both sides of the road. Thick concrete walls (piers) are built in a line between them.
▼

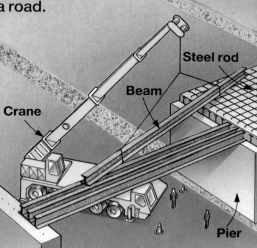

Crane

Beam

Steel rod

Concrete is poured out here.

Concrete pump

Abutment

Concrete is tipped in here.

Pier

Pier

Pier

Abutment

▲
2. A crane lifts concrete beams on top of the piers and the abutments.

▲
3. The builders lay a criss-cross of steel rods on top of the beams. Concrete is pumped on top of the rods.

Brick arch bridges

Arches

Bridges used to be built by making arches out of brick. Builders joined lots of arches together to make long bridges.

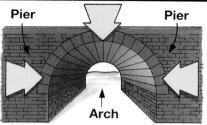

Pier

Pier

Arch

Brick arches are built between two thick brick piers. These stop the arch collapsing when weight is put on the bridge.

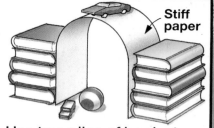

Stiff paper

Use two piles of books to keep a paper arch in place. The books will stop the arch from flattening even if you put a toy car on top.

Building over rivers

Building supports in a river is difficult and there are often wide gaps between them. Builders use several large concrete blocks to cross these gaps.

These strong wires help to stop the girder bending as the hoist travels along it.

The hoist travels along this girder.

Hoist

The blocks are floated towards the hoist on flat boats.

Support

Support

Concrete block

Concrete blocks are hollow inside.

A machine called a hoist lifts the blocks up to the bridge. The builders link them together with strong steel ropes called cables.

Boat

Strengthening the bridge

When all the blocks are in place, more cables are threaded through them. Steel plates are put on the ends of the cables to hold them in place.

A machine pulls the cables and squashes the blocks firmly together.

Concrete blocks

Cable

Steel plate

When blocks are joined like this, they will not fall apart, even when lorries go over them.

See how this bridge works

Squash a row of books together by pressing on the outside ones. You can lift them all up without touching the inside ones. Ask a friend to balance an object on top.

So long as you keep squashing the books together they will carry weight without breaking apart.

13

Suspension bridges

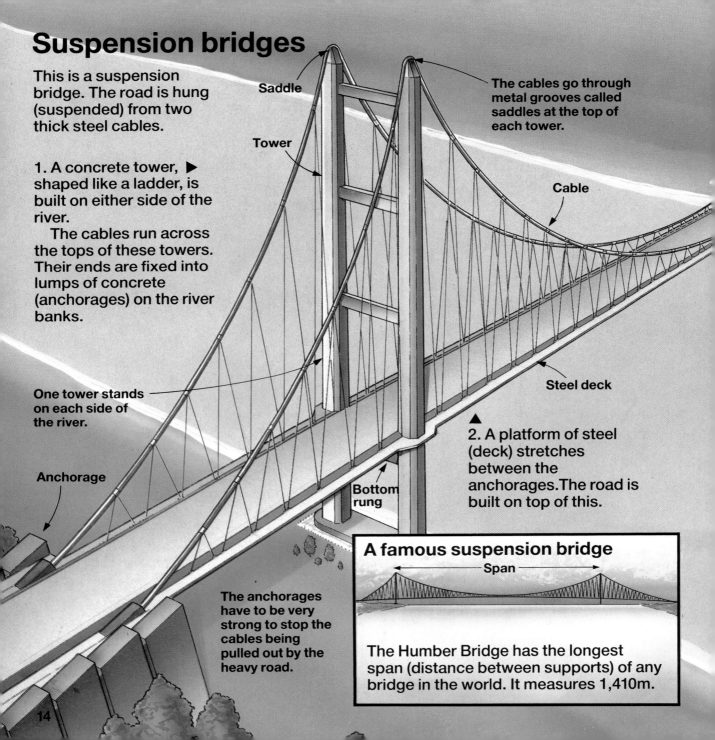

This is a suspension bridge. The road is hung (suspended) from two thick steel cables.

1. A concrete tower, ▶ shaped like a ladder, is built on either side of the river.
  The cables run across the tops of these towers. Their ends are fixed into lumps of concrete (anchorages) on the river banks.

Saddle

Tower

The cables go through metal grooves called saddles at the top of each tower.

Cable

Steel deck

One tower stands on each side of the river.

Anchorage

Bottom rung

▲ 2. A platform of steel (deck) stretches between the anchorages. The road is built on top of this.

The anchorages have to be very strong to stop the cables being pulled out by the heavy road.

A famous suspension bridge

← **Span** →

The Humber Bridge has the longest span (distance between supports) of any bridge in the world. It measures 1,410m.

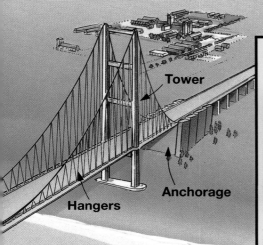

Tower

Hangers

Anchorage

▲
3. Hangers join the deck on to the cables. These hold the road up so that it doesn't bend or break.

Getting the deck in place

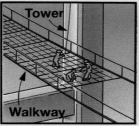

Tower

Walkway

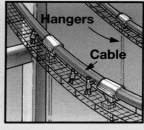

Hangers

Cable

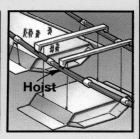

Hoist

1. Builders hang wire walkways between the towers. These are taken down when the bridge is finished.

2. They stand on the walkways to put the cables between the towers. They fix hangers to the cables.

3. A hoist lifts steel pieces up to the builders. They fix each piece to the hangers. This makes the deck.

Joining the deck together

When all the deck pieces are in place, some builders climb inside. They join pieces together with melted metal. This is called welding.

Here is how they do it:

1. They put metal rods in the gaps between the pieces.

2. They use electric power to melt the rods.

3. The melted metal fills the gaps. It hardens as it cools.

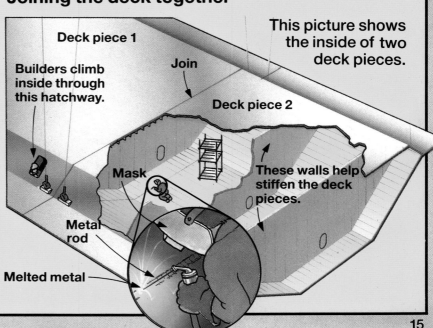

Deck piece 1

Builders climb inside through this hatchway.

Join

Deck piece 2

This picture shows the inside of two deck pieces.

Mask

These walls help stiffen the deck pieces.

Metal rod

Melted metal

Dams

Rivers overflow with water in winter but dry up in summer. Because of this, dams are built across rivers to store their water. A river blocked by a dam forms a huge lake called a reservoir.

Building the dam

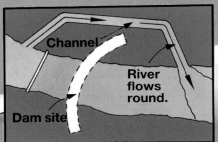

1. The builders blast underground channels through the valley's sides.

2. They use machines to dig out the river-bed until they reach a layer of solid rock.

3. They now build several tall concrete towers on the layer of solid rock. They spray cement into the gaps between the towers to make one enormous dam wall.

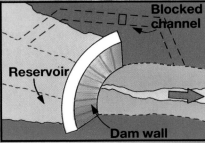

4. Finally, the underground channels are filled up with concrete. The river flows back until is blocked by the dam. A lot of water builds up to form the reservoir.

Reservoir

This dam has a curved concrete wall. It is called an arch dam. It can hold back billions of tons of water.

Valley

Power stations

When water flows fast it has a lot of power. This is turned into electricity in buildings called hydro-electric power stations.

These are built below dams where steep pipes can carry very fast-flowing water to them.

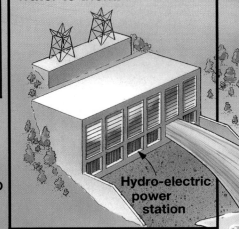

Hydro-electric power station

16

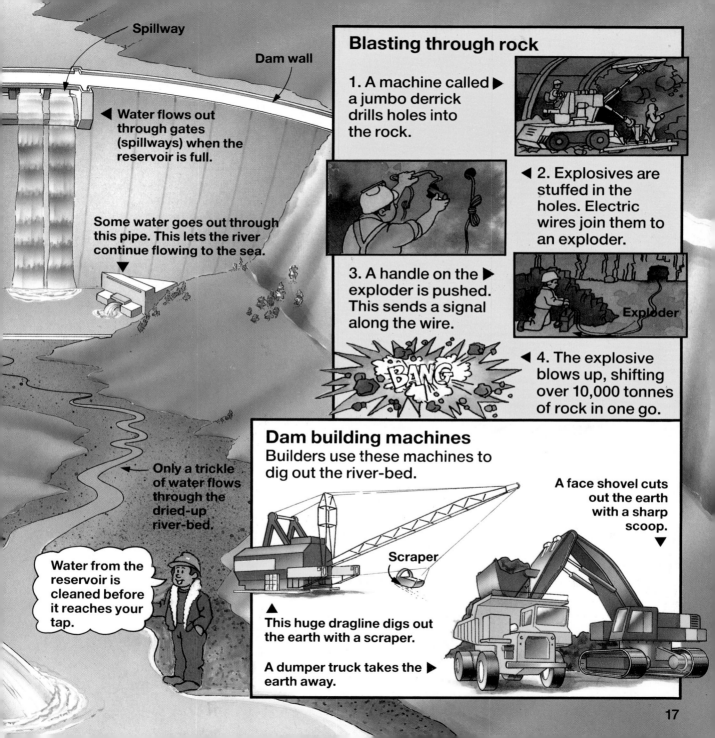

Spillway

Dam wall

◀ Water flows out through gates (spillways) when the reservoir is full.

Some water goes out through this pipe. This lets the river continue flowing to the sea.
▼

Only a trickle of water flows through the dried-up river-bed.

Water from the reservoir is cleaned before it reaches your tap.

Blasting through rock

1. A machine called ▶ a jumbo derrick drills holes into the rock.

◀ 2. Explosives are stuffed in the holes. Electric wires join them to an exploder.

3. A handle on the ▶ exploder is pushed. This sends a signal along the wire.

Exploder

◀ 4. The explosive blows up, shifting over 10,000 tonnes of rock in one go.

BANG

Dam building machines

Builders use these machines to dig out the river-bed.

A face shovel cuts out the earth with a sharp scoop.
▼

Scraper

▲
This huge dragline digs out the earth with a scraper.

A dumper truck takes the ▶ earth away.

Tunnels

Tunnels are built deep below cities, rivers, mountains and even the sea. Some are large enough for cars and trains to go through.

Large tunnels are made by this machine. It is called a TBM which stands for tunnel boring machine. It bores through the earth.

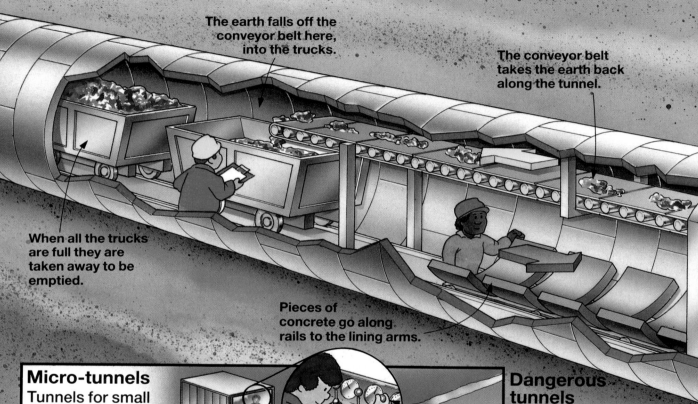

The earth falls off the conveyor belt here, into the trucks.

The conveyor belt takes the earth back along the tunnel.

When all the trucks are full they are taken away to be emptied.

Pieces of concrete go along rails to the lining arms.

Micro-tunnels

Tunnels for small pipes and drains are called micro-tunnels. Some micro-tunnels are dug by a machine called a remote-controlled drill. This is steered from a cabin on the ground above it.

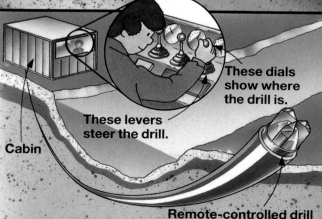

These dials show where the drill is.

These levers steer the drill.

Cabin

Remote-controlled drill

Dangerous tunnels

Freshly dug tunnels are often weak. Their sides could collapse, killing the builders. This TBM makes sure the tunnel does not collapse by lining the sides with concrete as it goes.

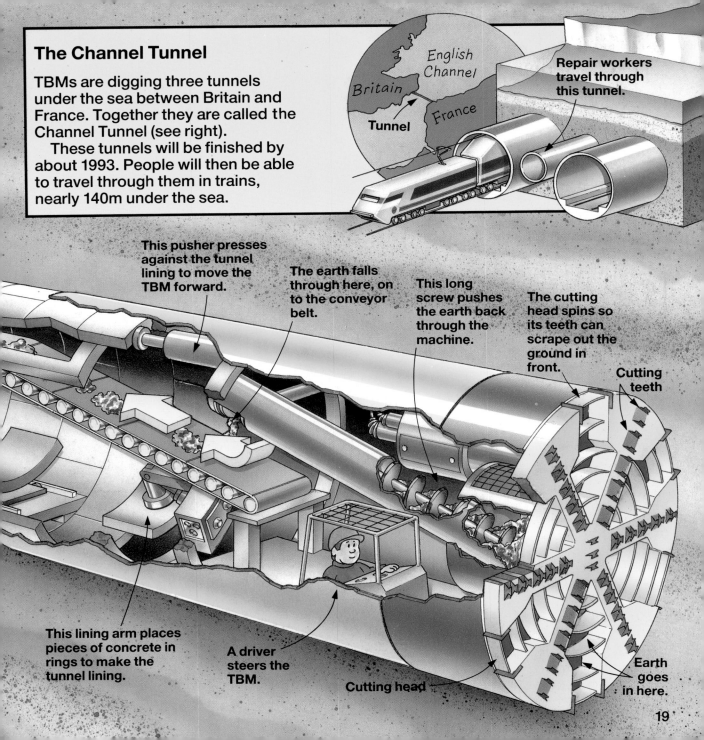

The Channel Tunnel

TBMs are digging three tunnels under the sea between Britain and France. Together they are called the Channel Tunnel (see right).

These tunnels will be finished by about 1993. People will then be able to travel through them in trains, nearly 140m under the sea.

English Channel

Britain

France

Tunnel

Repair workers travel through this tunnel.

This pusher presses against the tunnel lining to move the TBM forward.

The earth falls through here, on to the conveyor belt.

This long screw pushes the earth back through the machine.

The cutting head spins so its teeth can scrape out the ground in front.

Cutting teeth

This lining arm places pieces of concrete in rings to make the tunnel lining.

A driver steers the TBM.

Cutting head

Earth goes in here.

19

Offshore oil rigs

These rigs are drilling machines that get oil from under the sea. They are fixed to platforms which stand on the sea-bed. Over 100 people work on a platform. It must stand firm in rough seas to keep them safe.

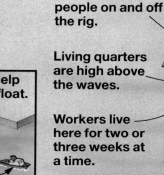

Building the platform

Gates keep out the sea.

1. Workers build the platform at a place near the sea called a dry dock.

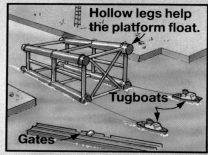

Hollow legs help the platform float.

Tugboats

Gates

2. Builders open the gates to let water into the dock. The platform is towed out to sea.

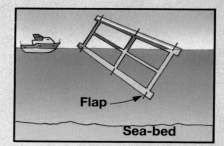

Flap

Sea-bed

3. Builders open flaps in the legs to let water in. The platform sinks and stands upright on the sea-bed.

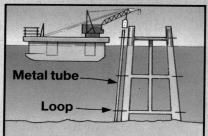

Metal tube

Loop

4. Tubes are hammered through loops on each leg. These go deep into the sea-bed to keep the platform in place.

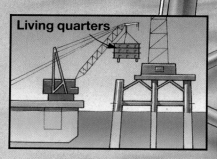

Living quarters

5. Boats carry out the rig and living quarters. A floating crane lifts them up on top of the platform.

Helideck

Helicopters land here to take people on and off the rig.

Living quarters are high above the waves.

Workers live here for two or three weeks at a time.

Platform

The platform rests on these long legs.

The legs are often more than 200m long.

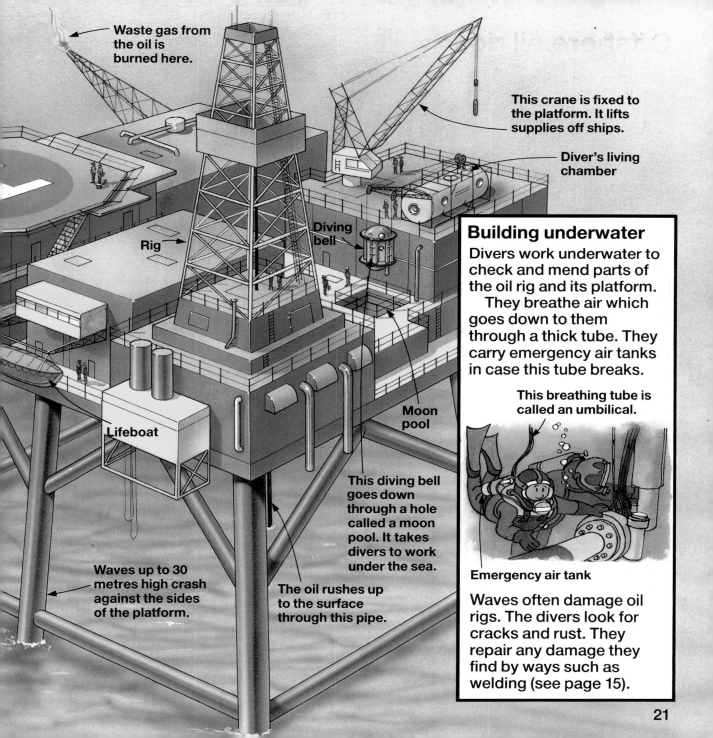

Waste gas from the oil is burned here.

This crane is fixed to the platform. It lifts supplies off ships.

Diver's living chamber

Rig

Diving bell

Building underwater

Divers work underwater to check and mend parts of the oil rig and its platform.

They breathe air which goes down to them through a thick tube. They carry emergency air tanks in case this tube breaks.

This breathing tube is called an umbilical.

Moon pool

Lifeboat

Emergency air tank

This diving bell goes down through a hole called a moon pool. It takes divers to work under the sea.

Waves up to 30 metres high crash against the sides of the platform.

The oil rushes up to the surface through this pipe.

Waves often damage oil rigs. The divers look for cracks and rust. They repair any damage they find by ways such as welding (see page 15).

21

What buildings are made of

Egyptians probably used cement in their pyramids.

Name	Where it comes from	What it is used for
Asphalt. Black, stony mixture.	It is made by mixing crushed rock with hot bitumen.	It is spread on roads to make a tough surface (page 11).
Bitumen. Thick, sticky oil.	Sometimes it seeps out of the ground. Sometimes it is drilled out by oil rigs.	It is mixed with crushed rock to make asphalt for roads.
Bitumenised felt. Black, waterproof material.	It is made by spreading bitumen on rough felt.	It is used to stop damp rising up walls (page 5).
Brick. A hard block of clay.	Clay is shaped into bricks. These are put into a hot oven (kiln) to harden them.	Bricks are used for building walls (page 5). Bricklayers stick them together with mortar.
Cement. Fine powder.	It is made from clay and chalk. These are mixed, burnt and then ground up.	It sticks sand and stones together. It is used in concrete and mortar.
Concrete. A type of man-made rock.	It is made by mixing sand, broken stones, cement and water. It sets hard when dry.	Concrete is used to make lots of things such as blocks, towers, columns and foundations.

The fastest bricklayer in the world is Ralph Charnock of Great Britain. He once laid 725 bricks in an hour.

Thousands of years ago, builders used bitumen to stick bricks together instead of mortar.

The tallest building in the world, the Warsaw Radio Mast, is made of steel. It is 646 m tall.

Name	Where it comes from	What it is used for
Mortar. Gritty paste which dries hard.	It is made by mixing sand, cement and water.	It is used to stick bricks together (page 5).
Plaster. Stiff paste which is hard and smooth when dry.	A rock called gypsum is ground to a fine powder and then mixed with sand and water.	It is spread over brick and concrete walls to make them smooth (page 7).
Plasterboard. Stiff board.	It is made by sandwiching plaster between two sheets of paper.	It is used to make ceilings and some inside walls (page 6).
Reinforced concrete. Very strong concrete.	It is made by letting concrete set around steel rods or bars.	It is often used to make bridges because it is so strong cars and lorries can go over it (page 12).
Steel. Very strong metal.	It is made from iron which has been heated in a type of very hot oven called a furnace.	Pieces of steel are joined together to make things such as bridges, oil rigs and skyscrapers.
Wood. The inside of a tree.	Trees are cut down and sawn up to make pieces of wood for building.	It is used to make floors and roof frames in many houses. Some houses are made just from wood.

Did you know that the largest concrete building in the world is the Grand Coulee Dam?

It is on the Columbia River, USA.

Index

Acknowledgements

We wish to thank the following people and organisations for their help: Transmanche Link, Gifford and Partners, Col. W. I. F. Austin, Jonathan Louth B.A. (Hons)Arch, Dip.Arch., Wharton Williams and Comex Houlder Limited.